T0064514

# Big Mystery of BAYSPORT

BONNIE HOWELL-LUTTON

A memorable experience.

authorHOUSE®

AuthorHouse™
1663 Liberty Drive
Bloomington, IN 47403
www.authorhouse.com
Phone: 1 (800) 839-8640

Published by AuthorHouse    07/24/2015

ISBN: 978-1-5049-2451-1 (sc)
ISBN: 978-1-5049-2450-4 (e)

Print information available on the last page.

Any people depicted in stock imagery provided by Thinkstock are models,
and such images are being used for illustrative purposes only.
Certain stock imagery © Thinkstock.

This book is printed on acid-free paper.

Because of the dynamic nature of the Internet, any web addresses or
links contained in this book may have changed since publication and
may no longer be valid. The views expressed in this work are solely those
of the author and do not necessarily reflect the views of the publisher,
and the publisher hereby disclaims any responsibility for them.

# CONTENTS

# The Move

The sun was slowly rising in the sleepy little town of BaysPort. Justin's awakened to the sounds of the sea gulls morning laughter. He could hear his mom in the kitchen, the smell of coffee brewing told him it was time to get out of bed. You really couldn't call what he slept in last night a bed, more like a make shift pallet. Tonight he would have his old bed to sleep in again; too bad it wasn't in his old room. He angrily thought!

"Rise and shine," moms' voice chimed as she walked down the narrow hall to the kitchen. We've got lots to do today. Mom seemed so happy this morning. Justin couldn't imagine why anyone could be so happy to be in BaysPort. If he had his rathers he would still be in good ole' Houston, not this speck on a map. "I can't believe life has come to this," he grumbled as he pulled on his shirt and shoes making his way to the kitchen. Mom had put out juice, coffee cake

1

and cereal for breakfast. She was already outside starting to unload the moving van. Tom was helping her. They had been married only four years and still they knew how to anticipate each other's thoughts and ideas.

To Justin it seemed like only yesterday that his mom and real dad was together. The past six years had been extremely hard for him. In those six years, he had watched his real dad walk out on him and his mom and to top it off he had left when mom was going to have his sister any day. His dad never even said goodbye. His sister Sandra was born prematurely and struggled for life, spending a month or more in the hospital. His mom had worked twelve hour days in a dry cleaner plant. Life had been that way until Tom came into the picture. Tom had been a family friend for some time. Once mom and dad were divorced, and mom experienced living on her own, with two kids, for over a year. Tom finally asked Justin's mom out, the rest as they say is "History." Justin had been happy in the big city and could see no reason to move here.

Boxes were being unloaded, furniture being carried into various rooms of the new house when a group of neighborhood kids gathered in the drive way. The kids happily welcomed Justin and his little sister Sandra. Before he knew it all the kids had pitched in and helped with the unloading. Several of the kid's parents made their way over welcoming Justin and his family to the neighborhood. As the day wore on Sandra played in the back yard on her swing set with some of her new found friends. Justin busied himself in his room, avoiding any chance of being asked to help out he really missed his friends at home.

No matter where I am Houston will always be home

he thought as he continued putting his new room together. Hours passed quickly, Justin's room was really shaping up. Well it's not where I want it to be, but it will do for now, but soon as I'm eighteen his thoughts trailed off. Shortly after four o'clock p.m. the doorbell rang, Sandra ran to answer it. At the door stood a young man about Justin's age, "Hi I'm Robert," is Justin done in his room yet?

Justin somebody's here for you, Sandra yelled down the hall. Come on in she offered to the boy, that's ok, I'll wait here he smiled. Justin finally cleared his doorway and made his way down hall to the living room. Hi, how's it going man? He greeted him. Alright, I guess Justin grumbled, want to go in my room and check it out? Sure, Robert followed him to his room. Man you sure got a lot of stuff, said Robert with amazement. My room is practically vacant compared to yours Robert joked! Yeah I got a lot of junk I guess, Justin replied. Good junk looks like from here Robert said trying to lighten the mood. Say man how much longer you got to go before you can come out and let me give you a tour of our stomping grounds around here? He questioned. Hang on I'll ask my mom to take a break for a while, Justin called out to his mom asking to go out for a while. She quickly said ok, but don't stay, gone too long, dinner time will be here soon. Alright mom, I'll be back in plenty of time Justin promised as her practically ran out the door.

You've already met most of the guys around here this morning when you were unloading, now it's time to go exploring a bit, Robert said with a wide grin. They hopped on their bikes and headed east towards the bay. They rode on talking guy talk and comparing life notes. Robert's parents were divorced too, so he knew some of Justin's feelings.

Roberts' mom had also remarried only less than a year ago. Robert's dad had remarried ten days after the divorce was final. Robert called his step-mom, mom and his real mom, mama. He admitted its' hard having step parents, but actually in his case his step-dad Frank was much better to him than his real dad ever had been. The boys rode their bikes on down the street till they came to a tiny cemetery. Robert turned off the road into the cemetery, come on he called over his shoulder to his new friend, this place is really awesome!

Justin followed his new friend fearlessly. Once inside the Gate they rode almost to the very back. Finally, Robert came to stop under a huge oak tree. This was the biggest tree Justin had ever seen. Let's rest here for a while suggested Robert. The tree set on top of a hill, you could see the bay go on for miles from here. Why did you bring me here asked Justin? This is my favorite place ever laughed Robert and let me tell you why....

Robert began his explanation. This place has been here forever. There are pirates and slaves buried here. Do you remember "Blue Beard" the pirate, he asked? I've heard of him before, Why, asked Justin? Are you going to try to creep-me out, asked Justin? No joking around Robert continued, this place really has a legend. See that huge oak tree over there?

Well legend has it that a treasure could be buried in it. Don't you mean under it Justin questioned? No, in it now explained Robert. See the tree has grown and the treasure grew up with it, understand, sort of asked Robert? Yeah, I guess Justin half-heartedly replied. Out of the corner of his eye Justin saw something moving in the low tree branches.

Suddenly out of the lowest branch jumped a lankly red-headed boy about the same age as Robert and Justin. Oh Robert you trying to convince somebody else of your hauntings? Hi! I'm David the boy stuck out his hand to Justin, with his thick southern accent he said.

Glad to meet cha! Hey guys came a call behind the boys, it was Paul, the kid from across the street, from Justin's new house. The boy from behind Justin's house, Mike was also walking up to them. See you've been introduced to our place Mike said with a wide grin, sort of returned Justin. They all sat on the ground under the tree. The evening was wearing on; the sun was beginning set over the bay. Robert returned to his story. My Grandpa says that pirates roamed all over the place. There was a certain pirate that called this port his own. Other Pirates feared him; he was the meanest pirate around. He was known as "Captain Barnicial, Earnest Barnicial." The sea breeze began to pick up, the trees made an eerie sound above them. Justin felt a slight chill move over him. He knew that there was no way, he could be cold. Robert continued. The Captain had only one weakness, her name was Cindy, she was very beautiful. She had long curly auburn hair, green eyes and lots of money and to go with that Cindy's father was a cattle baron, he owned the entire county. He was a very powerful man. The Captain tried to stay clear of Cindy's father, not because he was afraid of him.

The Captain knew how much Cindy loved her father and he couldn't bare, to hurt her in any way. He was in port on his ship when she and her family came by in their carriage along the harbor road. The Captain was totally spell-bound by Cindy's beauty. She looked directly at him and time stood still. Well anyways, that's how my Grandpa tells it. Grandpa says women have a way of turning a man's world upside down. Well anyways, the Captain began secretly courting the Baron's daughter. The two of them fell madly in love. They were very careful not to get caught, but one day it happened. Cindy and the Captain were caught in the garden of the Barons mansion, by her father. He was very angry; he banished her to the mansion. She had to have her governess with her at all times. Cindy's mother was very ill and passed on soon after the Captain and Cindy fell in love with each other. Cindy made daily trips to the cemetery.

Her mother's grave is right here under the tree. Robert pointed to the large head stone. The Captain would bury letters and treasures of gold, jewelry and stuff like that for her. Cindy would wait until her governess went to visit a family members' grave, before she would uncover what her Captain had left for her. After a while Cindy's father sent her off to Paris to boarding school. Her dad wanted her to be a distinctive young lady, cause one day she would be the owner of her father's empire.

Her father wanted her to marry a man who would carry on his business with all the dignity that he had. For this reason she had to go to Paris. Cindy wrote a letter to her Captain to explain. She waited for his reply. Each day she would check behind the headstone, finally a response came. The Captain said go, do what must be done. I will be here when you return. So she left for school. She stayed in Paris for a year.

She wrote letters to a friend who delivered them to the Captain. He sailed to Paris a couple of times, to surprise her. In the time that Cindy was in school a marriage was arranged by Cindy's father and the oil barrens son. When

Cindy returned home, there was a ball planned. At this ball, Cindy's father announced the engagement of his daughter to the oil barrens son. Cindy was heartbroken, but what could she do? The marriage was set.

A few days later she visited the cemetery, she was allowed to go alone. Her father was satisfied that she would honor his wishes not to see the Captain again. The captain saw her walking thru the cemetery from his ship and joined her. She told him of her father's plan of her marriage to oil Barons' son. That's when the Captain decided to pay her father a visit. The Captain and the Barron did meet and it wasn't pretty. The Captain tried to explain that he is no longer a pirate. The Baron refused to hear anything that the Captain had to say. The Baron threatened the Captain, that if he didn't leave his daughter alone, he would have him shot. It didn't matter that Captain was now working as a part of the Queen's fleet. Cindy was now promised to someone else. Captain vowed not to give up. Cindy again was sent away to Paris until the day of her wedding. About a month before the wedding, the Baron mansion was broken into and Cindy's father was confronting the intruder when he had a heart attack and died. One of the servants said she heard the Baron and the Captain arguing earlier that night, and the Captain said "he would live, die and kill for Cindy." So he was accused of coming back during the night breaking in and causing the Barron's death.

The captain had left days before to return to pirating the open seas. He never knew he had been accused of murder. Cindy went to the cemetery many times waiting under the trees for the captain, he never came. Cindy refused visitors; she spent most of her time in her father's observatory on the third floor. She spent many hours looking across the bay for the captain. One night a terrible storm blew in. The storm caused much damage. Cindy went up to the observatory to look over the bay at the damage done. To her horror, she saw the captain's ship in pieces.

The ship had been wrecked. That day she summoned a boat, to take her to the ship! Only half of the ship was above water. The captain was not on the boat. Several of his crew's bodies were on board. Later that week there were claims made of more of the captain's crew washed upon shore! Someone claimed to have found the captain's body. Cindy's heart was broken. Again she refused any visitors. She would come every day to the cemetery and wait, she left letters every day. No response ever came, no letters ever picked up. Her servants were afraid their young mistress wouldn't last much longer. She would return from the cemetery only to go to her room, refusing to eat or drink.

# THE LOSS

She sat by her window crying. Pretty soon the servant's fears came true. Cindy became very ill. Her aunt from New York came to care for her. The doctors couldn't figure out what was wrong with her. She died several weeks later. What nobody knows, was that the captain was still alive and had placed treasures for her in the mansions garden. He believed that she had married the oil Barron's son. The captain had sold his ship before the horrible storm and most of his crew went with the new owner. He now had a ship from the Queens fleet of his own. It had been nearly a year since he had visited the Port. He went to the mansion only to find Cindy's not there. Her aunt had large dogs he didn't expect. Their barks awakened Cindy's aunt, she carefully went down stairs with her pistol in hand.

She saw a shadow of a person and she shot him. "Shot him dead!" Her aunt had been plagued many nights by

Cindy's ghost searching and crying for the captain. Now the captain lay at the foot of the stair case dead. A few months went by and Cindy's aunt boarded up the mansion, and went back to New York, never to return. The house sitting high upon the hill over there was their home. The house was given to the town by her aunt. A lot of people moved in and out never staying long. The state turned it into a "Historical Site" a few years ago. Some people claim it's haunted they see people in it at night, hear music and see parties going on. On other nights people claim to hear a woman crying and wandering around the house and grounds. The house is open for tours but the third floor observatory stays closed. They say it's because it stays ice cold, and you can see and hear Cindy in the room. Some people even say they get an eerie feeling when they tour Cindy's bedroom.

Some fishermen claim they have seen the captain's ship and see a shadow of a figure go from the ship to the mansion and heard a man calling out for someone named Cindy. They also claimed to see a man with a shovel burying something behind a headstone in the cemetery. That's it: That's the story my grandpa told me and his grandpa's grandpa and grandma told him. It's a legend around here, Robert concluded. A long silence followed. Finally David, Mike, and Paul all at the same time made an eerie ooooooh, sound followed by laughter. Creepy, they chimed again. Stop it! You're just jealous because I know the legend. Besides I've seen things around here too. 'Robert explained.' The boy's sat there for a bit. So what do you think about it Justin? asked Robert.

I don't know, I don't believe in ghost and hauntings Justin replied, not to hurt your feeling, but maybe somebody made up all that a long time ago. I don't think so Robert broke in, you all will see. If you hang around long enough you will see. Speaking of hanging around we better get home before our folk's send out a search party for us, David said, as he stood up to leave the group. Right the boys agreed. Everyone parted ways except for Robert and Justin who rode their bikes home. They talked of school, girls, cars, things boys' talk of, they ended their conversation "with see ya!" That evening Justin was pretty quiet during dinner. Claiming to be tired he excused himself took a shower and went to bed. He went to sleep thinking about Robert's story. Just a dumb story he told himself. He dreamed of his move and of the story Robert told. In his dreams he saw the beautiful girl and her pirate.

# THE MYSTERY BEGINS

Night was over much too soon. Justin's alarm clock was an unwelcome sound. Monday morning was here, time to go to school. What would all the kids think of him? Justin wondered, as he quickly dressed. He wandered into the kitchen where mom and Sandra were finishing their breakfast. Breakfast smells good, Justin said in his sleepy voice.

Hurry and eat don't be late on your first day mom called! I've got to drop your sister off as school and get to work. Just put your dishes in the sink before you go, "Love you" mom called as she went out the door with Sandra in tow.

As Justin was leaving, Robert wheeled into the drive way on his bike. Taking your bike he called to Justin! I guess I could, returned Justin getting his bike out from the garage and locking the doors. The boys hurried to school. Once there Robert introduced Justin around. Robert and Justin had a few classes together, when they weren't together, Justin tried to lay low. The girls seemed very nice and friendly here, he only worried if they had boy's friends' of the jealous type. Justin's nerves settled as the day wore on. By lunch he was welcomed pretty well by all his peers. However, his deepest thoughts were still in Houston. His friends there were most likely having a great time as usual, just without him.

Something jolted his thoughts back to reality. Before he knew it the lunch table he had sat down at was filled up by new faces and those of his new found friends from his neighborhood. David, Robert and their friends seem nice enough. Lunch went by in a flash, along with the rest of the day. Justin in his heart did not want to be here. He kept going back to the fact. He kept telling himself, he wouldn't allow himself to be truly happy here. At the end of the school day the boys from Justin's neighborhood all rode their bikes home together. Little was said between the boys during the ride.

As Justin rode up into the yard, parking his bike in the garage, he could smell moms supper cooking. It enveloped him as he opened the door. Smells good! Justin called out to his mom as he made his way down the hall to his room. Sandra was in the back yard playing with a couple of the smaller kids of the neighborhood. The children's laughter came pouring through his open window, filtered only by the screen. Justin thought his room was finally taking shape. Supper was great. Mom's homemade pizza, everybody loved mom's pizza!

After supper was over as Justin, was putting the last dish in the washer, his friends rang the doorbell.

Robert and Paul wanted to know if Justin could come

out for just a little while. To his surprise mom said yes. Neat he thought, she would have never said yes in Houston. Maybe it might not be so bad here after all, he thought. The thought was quickly put away. Mom called as he headed out the door be back by 8 p.m., NO **LATER**! Cool he called back. The boys again on their bikes headed down towards the bay. Before they knew it they were back at the cemetery, back to the spot of the wild story of previous visits. The mansion sitting in the shadows of the pending darkness, with only lights from the front of it.

The sight was slightly eerie. The boys talked about boy things, girls, school, cars, boats just casual boy thoughts. In the distance Justin was sure he could see shadows. Just what those shadows were he wasn't exactly sure. Across the bay he could see a light fog rolling in. There, in the distance, he was almost sure he saw something. It was something it almost appeared to be a ship! Or not…Feeling kind of self-conscious, he looked to see if the guys saw it too. It was hard to read their faces. He looked out again, as he thought it was getting harder to tell just what he might be seeing. The fog was getting thicker. The bay and the mansion now had an eerie ora about them, getting lost in the mist.

Robert and Paul started talking about the mysteries surrounding the old house and the ghost ships or ship. The boys continued, it's a claim that on certain nights you can hear music coming from the old house, the old house was known in its days for many balls and celebrations. The Barren in his early days had much to celebrate and many riches to be proud of.

The boys talked on for what seemed like hours. There was a full moon just beginning to make itself known through the fog. Time had passed quickly. The boys decided that it was time to be heading back. Just as Justin, was about to get on his bike something caught his eye. It looked like a woman in the distance. It was hard to tell in the fresh fog and mist. Justin felt as if he were cemented to the ground, he just simply couldn't move. He tried to speak; he could only stare at the vision before him in the distance. Justin felt suddenly weak in the knees. All he could do was continue to stare at who ever, or whatever it was coming closer to him. He couldn't say if the guys were still there with him, or if they had rode off towards home. Had they gone and left him alone to face whatever it was? She was getting closer or appeared to be, was he dreaming all this?

As he stood there he began to feel a chill moving over him. She was there! Yes she was! She was so close to him, he could almost reach out and touch her, or could he?

Her face was a vision of beauty, by far the prettiest girl he had ever laid eyes on. Her eyes were the bluest of blue, that Justin had ever seen. He felt as if he could get lost in her eyes. She was staring right through him, or was she? A smile was on her face, as if she was looking into the face of her best friend. Was she looking at him? He tried to turn around to look behind him. No way, why couldn't he move? In the blink of an eye she was gone, just as she had appeared. It was all a mystery. The guys were on their bikes yelling from the gate way of the cemetery. "Let's go," they were trying to wait on their lagging friend. What's up with you? They called. Nothing, nothing, just got my pant leg stuck in the bike chain, Justin lied. Justin decided not to say a word about what he just saw.

Unless they say they saw it first.

He didn't want they guys to think he got all wimpy and creeped out by their ghost stories, legends, tall tales, whatever. The boys were in too big of a hurry to speak to each other on the ride back to their houses. They just told each see ya' tomorrow. Justin was home, but still felt creepy somehow. He closed the blinds and put down the windows in his room. He took the quickest shower in his personal history. He was so shaken by the sights of tonight it would be hard to sleep for sure!

It was all he could think of getting ready for bed. He jumped in bed, put his headphones on and decided to jam till he could fall asleep. Sleep, sleep, at last came for Justin. Night quickly became day. The sound of an alarm clock and the smell of the morning meal waiting was Justin's cue to get moving. For some strange reason this morning he was feeling eager to get to school. "Weird" he thought.

He quickly dressed joining the family in the kitchen. As he entered the kitchen everyone exchanged morning greetings. Mom was so big into family meal times, always had been.

Justin couldn't help but see how happy his mom seemed to be here. He only wished he could share in her joy. Mom, Sandra and Tom were all eating and chatting happily. Justin tried to join in. He wanted to be a happy family, really he did. Just with dad, a happy family with dad. He attempted to join in eating a bit too fast for mom. She gave him that slow down where's the fire look, so he slowed a bit. Suddenly he heard the bus horn. Gotta go, riding the bus today. Justin scarfed down the last of his breakfast. He was out the door and gone. He ran up the bus steps, stumbling onto the bus. He heard a few snickers as he made his way to the seat next to Robert, David and Paul. Morning sunshine, chuckled Paul. So tell me again why we are riding the big yellow twinkee this morning and not riding our bikes, Justin inquired. Don't you ever watch the news? Robert asked. No why should I, there's never anything good in it. Ever pick up a newspaper Robert asked in the same dull tone? Nope same reason Justin said, never anything good!

That's in the big city boy; things are different in a small town. You still haven't answered my bus question, Justin protested. Look around you, see that blinding sunshine his two friends' nearly sang out in tune. It's going to rain today, ever rode your bikes around in a rainstorm? I'd rather ride the thing you call a twinkee! All three boys agreed. Besides look at all the babes. Yep the bus is good sometimes, Paul suggested. The bus had made lots of stops and was now full. They were circling back around to head out if the subdivision. That's when Justin noticed the mansion. It looked so lonely and creepy even in the daylight, he thought. He almost thought he felt a creepy chill. He didn't let on. After all the guys would think he was stupid, or wimpy!

Justin was beginning to feel a little more at ease in the school. His old school was not as big; it was only a ninth grade center. Here ninth through twelfth was in the same school. Crazy he thought. He would have been in the High School in Houston, that next year any way's. He would have been just as nervous, there and with all rights to be. It was a known fact that the high school, he would have went to had lots of gang activity in it. Enough of that he thought crossly, just as the bell rang. Great now I'm late figures. His math class was his first class of the day, and the worst! He slipped inside the room amoungust all the chatter and morning confusion. Awe how convenient he thought. No one said a word about him walking in after the bell. Cool he thought. A good day begins.

Before Justin knew it, lunch time was there. He met up with the guys, Robert, David and Paul at their regular table. He knew this because the guys had told him that you pick a place to sit at first when you get in the school and stay there and for the most part everyone stays to their area. This just seemed to be the way things work. Everyone was chowing down. The girl's were giggling, and the guys were girl watching. Just a normal day in a high school lunchroom. The rest of the day flew by.

True to Robert, David and Paul, predictions, the sky grew dark with rain clouds. A storm blew in at one o'clock p.m. As the boys exited their last class of the day they were glad they chose to ride the bus today. Justin ran to the bus to find his buddies already there. The bus was noisy on the way home. Justin was so tired, he said very little on the trip home.

The boys stop was second one on the route. Thankfully the ride was a short one. Robert asked to come home with Justin as his mom was still at work. Sure, "come on" Justin called over his shoulder. Justin's mom didn't get off work for another half hour, and besides she wanted him to have friends. As long as we go to my room and don't wreck the house, my mom will be cool with you at our house. David and Paul quickly disappeared to their own houses. We got chores, see ya' later when we are done they called after Justin and Robert. The boys were all gone in a flash. Justin went into the kitchen and put a bag of popcorn in the microwave and poured two tall glasses of milk for them.

The boys settled in Justin's room at his desk to work on their homework. Justin remarked, the weather is as crazy here as in Houston. I guess was the only reply from Robert. As the boys were finishing up their homework, they heard Justin's mom and Sister Sandra enters the house. Sandra couldn't be missed. She was loud for a little girl. The rain seems to be just a mist now Robert remarked! Yeah I see that replied Justin. Want to go to my house in a few questioned Robert? Sure I guess returned Justin. I have to check with my mom and see if she needs me to do anything first.

The boys headed to the kitchen. Hi mom, Justin greeted her as he entered the kitchen where mom had already started cooking supper. Hi, how was your day mom called cheerily as she continued to cook.

Alright I suppose both boys chimed together. A regular school day retorted Justin. Hey mom can I go over to Robert's dog. I suppose it would be okay but call and check in, in a few to see if supper is ready. With that Robert grabbed the trash and Justin grabbed the dog food. Soon as the chores was done, they headed for Robert's place. Justin called over his shoulder to his mom see ya later! Okay mom returned, try to stay out of the rain. okay mom. The boys chuckled as they ran out the door Robert's house was a lot like Justin's. Seem like all the houses in this town were made a lot alike inside. That is unless you live in the country club or in the or in the Yacht clubs subdivisions.

The boys ran to Robert's house it was only misting rain now. Robert said he had lots of video games. Justin was more than ready to try them out. Friend's games were always a lot more fun than yours. Robert unlocked the door quickly as possible. They streaked through the house and up the stairs.

This is my room boasted Robert as he threw open the door. There inside was the evidence of a young teen age boy's room. Car posters, baseball posters, video games, football, baseballs, soccer balls, the whole nine yards! Great room Justin proclaimed just can't find the floor. Is there carpet or tile? Justin teased. Very funny just wait yours will look the same soon. Yep I supposed, Justin laughed.

The boys played video games and listened to the stereo. When the boys took a break Justin looked out of Robert's window "cool view," he exclaimed. Yeah it's okay I guess, was Roberts only reply. Justin could see the cemetery and the mansion from here.

It had a very eerie look to it still thought Justin. The boys heard Roberts's mom calling "I'm home," as she came in the front door. Hey mom Robert called I'm in my room and Justin is here too. Okay, his mom answered.

Have you done your chores she questioned? Just about to Robert answered. Stay here and I'll be done in a few minutes, Robert instructed. I could help you Justin offered. Naw it's all good got it, said Robert as he left the room. Ok. agreed Justin. He still hadn't moved from the window. His mind wandered off. I wonder what it was like to live there? He thought.

# THE MYSTERY

As he was gazing at the mansion, he could have sworn he saw somebody in the garden. Oh come on he told himself, somebody in a garden in the rain? No way! Still something was moving down there. He looked on. It looked like a woman in an old timey dress. Then there was another figure a man maybe. If it was a man he sure was dressed funny. Just then, there was a flash of lightning. Justin jumped back from the window, for a moment. Geez! He thought where did that come from? Still curious Justin moved back up to the window, were they, them, or it's, still there in that garden? He looks curiously again. Something or somebody was still there rain, lightening and all. Now it looked as if two people were hugging, dancing or something.

Justin couldn't seem to tare himself away. The wind had picked up now. He could also see the bay just past the mansion. What the heck he said out loud? It looked like a huge sailboat just sitting out in the bay. It was swaying back and forth with each gust of wind. Justin was mesmerized. There seemed to be movement on the boat or whatever that was out there. This is crazy, Justin thought. He looked back at the mansion where the two people were or whatever they were that he had seen. Humph not there now he thought to himself. Just then Robert came bouncing in the bedroom. Booooh! He called out. Justin jumped man. What the … look at you dude all pale and crap. You okay man? Dude, sorry if I scared you. What's up with you? Looking a little pale! Huh? Oh no just thinking and not expecting you. You got me good, explained Justin! Thinking? About what? Robert asked? Oh you know home, family, Houston, you know stuff. Alright man you're getting to deep now man. Okay agreed Justin.

The boys played for about thirty minutes then Justin decided to call home and check in. Mom said be home by seven-thirty p.m. for supper. Ok mom agreed Justin, see you then bye. I've got an hour till I have to be home. Cool let's play. At seven-thirty p.m. Justin put down his controller and announced, I better get going, mom gets ticked if I'm late. He walked back over to the window where he had stood before witnessing whatever, it was he thought. He could see the mansion and the bay. If there was anything there it sure is gone now he thought! Creepy. Robert and Justin took the stairs' two at a time down. At his front door Robert said "see ya' tomorrow man." see ya' Justin called back as he ran across the yard on to the street and to his front yard. Once he got to his door he waved to his friend.

He turned to look towards the bay just before he went inside. He felt a cold chill. Stupid rain he thought. Everyone was at home, and his mom was impressed he was actually early back from a friend's house for once. Suppers ready she called. The supper table was filled with idle chatter about everyone's day. When supper was over mom, cleared the table and put away the leftovers.

Kids it's your night for dishes. Justin and Sandra made their way to the kitchen. Neither was too thrilled to do dishes but, they did them. Sandra ran to the shower first.

Justin went to his room. He seemed to be drawn to the window as if someone was calling come look! He could see the bay, mansion from his room also, just not a second story view. It looked almost as if there was a dim light or candles inside the mansion, humph! He thought soon as he heard Sandra's bedroom door shut, he went to take his shower. After his shower Justin went to his room and fell across his bed looking at his ceiling. He must have dozed off. He woke suddenly as if he had been awakened by some body. He slowly looked around the dark room. Mom must have turned off his television.

What time is it he wondered, eleven-thirty p.m. Awwh crud!! He thought, why am I awake now? He turned back over after looking at his alarm clock. Laying there he thought he smelt something. He did, it was a sweet flowery smell. He sat up on the side of his bed. Justin suddenly felt a chill. A chill in August? This is stupid he thought, I must be dreaming he tried to convince himself. Suddenly he heard a very faint sound. It almost sounded like a woman humming softly. His mom hummed sometimes, but not now after eleven p.m. at night. He stood up crossed the room opening his door. The lights were all out everyone was asleep except for him or was he! He lay's back down on his bed. If he was awake he would go back to sleep. If he was asleep well he would, oh whatever he thought angrily.

The sweet smell seemed to get closer, the humming came closer too. The rustling sound of someone coming near him began. Justin laid still hoping his dream would either end or his encounter would end soon. He closed his eyes tight, waiting, waiting, still he really wanted to know who or what was there.

He must have fallen asleep waiting. The alarm suddenly rang and Justin shot up to turn it off. Man what a crazy night he exclaimed to himself! He opened his closet to start to dress, for school. He could hear his family already up and about in the rest of the house. He turned to cut off the fan on his dresser noticing the window was opened just a little. There on the dresser laid a jasmine flower. "What the heck?" he said out loud picking up the flower he made his way to the kitchen. Good morning called mom. Oh you brought me a flower she teased. Yeah well, he stammered, did you leave this in my room? No not me, mom laughed. Sandra did you put this in my room? No silly, Sandra exclaimed! Why would I give you a flower? Okay weird, I thought somebody was playing a trick on me. Not us mom and Sandra both said at once. Creepy weird thought Justin. Tom had already left for work. Maybe Tom had put it in his room for a practical joke. Justin decided to ask him tonight. That was it, Tom was the only answer. It was time to head off to school. The plan was to ride bikes today.

Justin was taking his bike out of the garage when Robert, David and Paul rode up in the driveway.

Let's go man we're going to be late. Off the boys rode! Justin tried to put the flower and craziness of last night out of his mind. School went by same as usual. Still Justin couldn't seem to shake the events of the night before. On the way home Robert questioned? "Hey man what's up with you?" You home sick or something? Naw man just tired didn't sleep much last night! Justin gave a tired huff. You want to come over later? Robert offered. Maybe Justin called back to Robert. I'll get a snack do the homework thing and all then I might.

Okay see ya man replied Robert, as he got off his bike and wheeled it in the yard. Robert knew he had chores and homework too. What a drag he thought as he unlocked his front door and went inside. Once Justin was inside he immediately made a trip to the fridge for a snack. There was a note on the fridge "gone grocery shopping be back soon", mom. Ok he thought house to self! He ate his snack got a big glass of milk. He parked himself at the kitchen bar and opened his science book. As he began to read he felt himself getting so sleepy. I'll lay my head down for just a few minutes then I'll work he thought to himself.

There it was again, that smell, that sweet flower smell. Where is it coming from? The faint humming song again. Hello is somebody there Justin called! Walking from the kitchen through the living room down the hall, towards his room. The sound and smell seemed to get stronger. Hello, anybody there? He called again," His room was filled with the smell, but empty. This is nuts he thought to himself as he headed back down the hall to the kitchen. The house was cool, and quiet, and had a mysterious feel to it. As Justin rounded the end of the bar he heard a rustle in the kitchen! The humming was soft, and sweet the aroma of flowers gets' stronger.

Justin remained quiet following the path the humming and scent made. He passed through the kitchen out the side into the garage. Where was he being lead? Justin hadn't a clue, but he followed. What was leading him and why? He could now hear his name being called softly. "Justin" he, could also hear himself, answer "I'm here" Where are we going?" The only answer was a single word "come". Justin felt as if he were floating instead of walking. Then suddenly out of no-where he heard his name being called, but not in a whisper this time. He felt as if he were falling or being pulled backwards. Justin, Justin, wake up! His mom called as she rubbed his back. He began to wake up saying "No, no don't go!"

He had the most sorrow filled feeling as he completely woke up. His mom was questioning him, "Are you ok?" Yes, yes, fine I think so," he slowly drawled as he become aware that he had fallen asleep. It must have been a dream he thought slowly as he shook the sleep from his thoughts. His mom was still watching him. Long day she questioned? Naw Justin said just boring science home work. Mom laughed as she ruffled his hair.

Grabbing his books he decided to finish his homework later, dumping them on his bed in his room he couldn't help thinking of that dream or whatever it was. Mom was calling, "could you take out the trash please?" Back in the kitchen he gathered the trash and headed out the side door same as he had went out in his dream. As he walked through the garage to the outside door to the back yard, he was still thinking of the voice and sweet smell.

As he reached for the lid on the big trash can, his hand

came in contact with more than the lid. Jerking his hand back he quickly dropped, the bag to the ground. There on the lid lay another jasmine flower. Justin began to back up. This is just too weird he thought. He turned and ran back in the house. Swinging the door wide nearly plowing his mom over. Hey, hey, where's the fire she exclaimed? Mom! Mom! Justin rushed come here, come with me, hurry! He practically pulled mom behind him. They hurried from the house through the garage out the back door to the outside trash can where the trash lay on the ground. On the trash can lid lay the flower. "Look mom look; he cried another one. His mom picked the flower up raising it to her nose, taking in the sweet smell. One of my favorites as mom sniffed in the fragrance once more. But mom how did it get here? Where did it come from he stammered, sounding shaken and confused?

Calm down his mom reassured him it had to come from somebody check with your friends. "No mom, guys don't leave flowers for other guys that's just creepy! Justin explained. Well, mom trying to come up with and explanation, reasoned, maybe there's a girl in the neighborhood that's trying to meet you.

That's even more gross, than one of the guys putting it there, yuck mom that's a strange way to meet someone. Not to a girl, mom smiled as she took the flower and proceeded back inside to her kitchen to cook supper. This is crazy, grumbled Justin, as he dropped the garbage in the can and went back inside the house. Meeting his sister in the hall, she began singing, Justin's got a girlfriend, Justin's got a girlfriend and don't even know who she is! Sandra teased him till he went into his room and shut the door, in disgust.

Maybe it's Sandra playing tricks on him. I better not find out he said out, loud as he flopped down on his bed. He decided to study again, till mom called him for supper.

After supper, it was his and Sandra's turn again to rinse dishes, load washer and wipe down counters and table. Justin gave her the easy job he thought. Sandra did the counters and tables. He asked his sister, "so where you getting the flowers you been leaving around?" 'Sandra stopped looked at her brother and began laughing. No way bro it's not me she, chuckled on. Why in the world would I leave you flowers she jokes? Like mom said she retorted there's some stupid girl somewhere round there that thinks your "hot! Stop it!" Justin grimaced as he finished his chore.

Sandra started her little Justin's got a girlfriend chant again exiting the kitchen and running down the hall to her room. That's right you better run girlie Q. Justin laughed as she shut her door. Justin was too tired for anymore studying. He got a shower and went to bed. Laying there he could hear the house hold winding down for the night. No dreaming he told himself as he felt himself drifting off to sleep. Sure wish this was my old room in my old house with mom and dad both here. "I miss you dad," was his last thought as he hit slumber town.

The annoying sound of the alarm clock shook Justin out of a peaceful sleep. Awe man isn't it Saturday yet? He murmured, as he drug himself from his bed. Getting dressed going to the kitchen in a foggy daze he smelled breakfast cooking. He dropped himself into the dining room chair and picked at his breakfast. Soon mom was reminding everyone of the time, like she did each weekday morning.

Feeling like the energy had been drained right out of

him he slowly moved across the kitchen to scrape out his plate and rinse it in the sink. I think I'll ride the bus today he grumbled. T.G.I.F. called mom after him as he went out the front door. Robert, David and Paul were walking up the drive way. "Bike or bus?" Robert asked as he walked up to greet Justin. "Bus." groaned Justin. Just then the bus rolled to a stop at the end of the driveway. The other boys jogged up to the bus, but not Justin, he was too tired for that. "They will just have to wait for me" he murmured under his breath.

The school day couldn't go by fast enough for Justin. The thought of tomorrow being Saturday was how he got through his day. He could have sworn that he had nodded off several times today in class. Why am I so tired he questioned? He had even put his head down just to close his eyes for a minute at lunch today. He spent most of his time reassuring people he wasn't sick. Even though he wasn't so sure he hadn't caught a bug or something. Robert had invited him to go for a bike ride to the bay to do a little fishing but he didn't think he would ... somehow a nap after school seemed more appealing. Friday evening and all he wanted was sleep! Weird he mused as he walked in his front door dropping his door key on the table in the hall. He headed straight to his room and lay down on his bed staring at the ceiling. Soon he was fast asleep. Suddenly he awoke to Tom, and his mom voices.

# THE MYSTERY DEEPENS

The noise of his family coming in the house woke him up. Mom, Tom and Sandra were sitting in the livingroom. It was already dark outside Justin noticed as he entered the living room looking out the window. "Wow, how long did I sleep?" He asked nobody in particular? Mom answered it is nearly seven-thirty. You were sleeping so sound we left you to your rest. There's pizza in the oven on warm mom chimed. "Pizza, my favorite!" he exclaimed as he pulled the boxes from the oven, making himself a lofty plate and pouring some ranch dressing on the side. He sat down at the table. Sandra was playing with her barbies. Mom and Tom were watching something or another on tv, stopping once in a while to joke about another commercial that made little to no sense.

Tom called to Justin in the dining room, "hey bud, you feeling rested yet"? Justin chuckled back, "yeah for now".

You should Sandra threw in, we could hear you snoring through the door. "I don't snore" Justin shot back, do I? he quickly questioned. Mom, Tom and Sandra all answered at the same time "Oh yes you do!" Feeling embarrassed he gobbled down his pizza. Can I go to Roberts's house he asked as soon as he was done? For a little while mom agreed but check back in by 9pm. Thanks mom, and with that Justin was out the door.

Knocking on Robert's door, Justin was hoping that he hadn't decided to do something else with the other guys since he had crashed so early. Robert opened the door with a wide grin. "He lives!" Robert teased as he motioned Justin in. "Man I went out when I got home, I just woke up about thirty minutes ago" Justin exclaimed, following Robert to his room, briefly speaking to Roberts family as he passed by them. Robert commented you still look kinda worn down, you sure you're alright? Yeah I'm ok, Justin shrugged.

The boys sat down for a few minutes. Robert picked up his guitar and softly strummed it as he asked, Justin what he wanted to do tonight, watch a movie, play a video game?, go fishing? Fishing sounds good Justin replied. Ok great man. Let's ask our parents. They went back to the living room and Robert got his permission while Justin went to ask his mom. Soon Justin was crossing the street with rod and tackle in hand. Where's your bike, his friend wanted to know. How am I suppose to get all this stuff to the pier on a bike, Justin quizzed. Just get your bike and follow the fish master, Robert joked. So Justin did just that.

Together they rode down to the pier on the Bayfront. Let the fishing begin teased Robert. Out went there first cast of the night. Neither boy got a bite for a while. They started talking and somehow got back on the subject of the mansion on the hill and pirate legend. Do you ever go to the mansion? Justin asked his friend.

"When I first moved here I practically lived there, now not so much. Why do you ask Robert wanted to know? Have you been there yet Robert asked Justin? No, Justin shook his head, I've only been here six days remember. They both laughed. About that time Robert's line gave a jerk. He jumped up to reel it in. It was a huge hard head fish Robert said. Never heard of a hard head fish before, Justin said laughing. I got to see this.

The fish came up none too happy making an angry let me go sound. Robert was fast to oblige him. Fish hit the water splat and was gone. An hour passed with little or no action. Robert stood up stretching. "Man this bites" he complained. Wonder where the specks are tonight? His friend Justin was staring off into the distance at the mansion. "Dude you want to go check it out?" quipped Robert. Without taking his eyes off the house Justin said sure man if you want. With that they got their fishing gear together, got on their bikes and headed to the old house.

The house was even bigger than Justin had thought. Even though the moon was full and bright the grounds seemed dark somehow. The house had a soft yellow glow in some of its windows. The house was locked so they couldn't go in. Slowly they walked around the huge house and grounds. Robert wanted to check out the basement where the cooking used to be done, just to see if it was open. The doorknob turned and clicked open. The basement was pitch, dark but Robert had his mini lantern in hand. They crept through the door and inspected the area under the huge house.

# MYSTERY SOLVED

It seemed to take forever to get across and back to the door of the basement. They stopped, each boy shushing the other and questioned, did you hear that? The boys could have sworn they heard music and what seemed like a party in the house, but the closer they got to the door the more faint it became. No explanation for it. They were almost at the door when a gust of wind from nowhere blew through followed by a hard thud! Oh no was that the door slamming, they both screamed. Just then Roberts's lantern went out. Just great Robert complained. What next quimmed Justin. In the dark no light and a door that just slammed shut, probably locking. Great, great Justin thought.

Both boys were groping around in the dark trying to find their way out. Suddenly it was bone chilling cold in the basement. Neither boy wanted to admit they were cold or even just a little bit nervous. After all, you can't let a buddy know things like that. Finally, they made it to the door. Both boys pulled on the door as hard as they could. It was no use! The door wasn't going to open from the inside by any means.

Justin was digging in his pockets for his phone. "Dang, I left my phone in my backpack on the bike" Justin confessed. Mine is my tackle box, Robert added. Well what a couple Einsteins we are, Robert laughed. Robert started to move around making his way to one of the windows that had some sort of metal cover on it. Maybe he could work it loose and they could get out, but even it wouldn't budge either.

While they were trying to figure out something else to do, the boys heard the roll of thunder. Awe man, not rain, no! they both chided. Soon they could see faint flashes of lightening then the pouring rain. Both boys knew their phones would be goners, but couldn't do anything about it.

It seemed like minutes were hours to them. Justin began to worry his mom would be worried sick if he wasn't home soon. Nobody knew they were here. What if their parents went to look for them on the peir, with the storm, had they already been there? Were they looking for them? Had everyone gone to sleep? All kinds of thoughts raced through his head. Man what a mess he cursed to himself.

The boys were both sitting near the door when both heard the rustling sound that seemed as if it was moving towards them. There was the smell of those flowers again. Justin wiggled closer to his friend. "Dude you hear anything?" he questioned his friend. "Yes!" Robert whispered his answer. What do we do Justin whispered back. Shhh!! His fiend coaxed, sit still and let's see what it is. Now the boys were sitting back to back. Each boy was straining their eyes to see anything. Justin could hear the sound, it was almost in front of him and a soft humming sound had joined the whishing sound, cold air surrounded both boys.

The sweet smell was assaulting his senses. Justin felt the need to shut his eyes tight, but he couldn't seem to move anything. He felt as if something or someone was right there in front of him. Almost like a cold breath on his face. He could feel goosebumps growing on him. As the boys sat there spell bound, a soft light began to appear, and they boys scooched closer together. Justin cracked a whisper, "look." Robert turned his head whispering, "I see it too." Soon both boys saw the unmistakable aspiration of a beautiful woman. She was leaning over looking closely at them. Neither boy spoke a word.

The woman stopped humming, placed her finger to her mouth whispering "shhh." With her other hand she motioned for Justin to follow her. He didn't want to move. A power he didn't recognize took over as he got up starting to follow this floating woman all the while dragging his friend behind him. The dim glowing light that surrounded her lit their way in the darkness. Both boys followed closely never saying a word, eyes fixed on the direction they were moving. Neither knew where or why they were following her. They must have traveled the entire length of the basement when they came to a stop. The boys could faintly see the loose metal covering on the basement vent flow opening.

It began to rattle, then, fell to the floor. She floated aside pointing to the opening. Then the humming started again. Her entrancing aroma made the boys feel at ease as they crawled through the tiny opening. Outside everything was drenched, and the rain, was still falling down. The boys had come out on the backside of the mansion. Both looked up to it. There was a light golden glow coming from the house. They could hear music ever so faintly. Justin and Robert climbed the back stairs to look inside the house.

There before their eyes they saw people dressed in old timey clothes, dancing, eating and talking. "What??" both boys said at once. Both began beating on the door. The people inside never reacted, as if they had never heard the pounding on the door. The scene continued. Behind them someone was whistling. Both boys whirled around to see nothing at all. "Who whistled?" they demanded! Just then lightening flashed and both wide eyed young men saw a man in the garden. The boys waved their arms and yelled to the man. Strangely enough he didn't seem to hear them either. Just like the folks inside the house.

They could hear him whistling a tune, why couldn't he see or hear them? Maybe it was the rain blocking them out. They both started for the steps but stopped short… A small floating bouncing light was heading in the direction of the strange man who was now holding his hat in his hand with its long feather being beaten by the steady rain. Robert and Justin froze in their tracks, watching the what was unfolding before their eyes. The moving light materialized into the woman they had encountered in the basement. It was the angel of mercy that had freed them earlier, but what was she doing in the garden in the rain with that man with the crazy looking hat?

They could hear the sound of her humming again. Still watching silently in the shadows, the boys bore witness to the two people in the garden as they realized that the other was there. They looked as if they were running to each other, they embraced as if they knew each other. The man, letting his hat fall to the rain soaked ground. They held hands as he retrieved his hat. They strolled through the rose garden as if it was something they must have done many times before. They strolled back towards the house facing the boys. They raised their hands waving to Justin and Robert. Dumb founded, the boys waved back. Another flash of lightening and a clap of thunder and they were gone.

Justin and Robert looked wearily at each other. One questioned the other at the same time, "what the heck just happened?" Both rubbed their foreheads, but neither could explain. In the distance they could hear people calling their names loudly. At the same moment, a bright light shown on the porch in their faces blinding them. Then came a voice from an unknown source. "Over here!" it commanded. "I found your boys!" Soon the lawn and garden area was busy with voices and people. The boys recognized the voices of their moms and siblings. Despite the pouring rain the boys ran out to meet their parents.

There were hugs, tears, and millions of questions. All hearts were full and grateful. The boys didn't know if they should tell all, in fear of everyone thinking they were making up stories, so they left the story at getting caught in the rain and running to the mansion for a safe dry place. Just then both boys remembered their bikes, phones and gear that had been left out in the storm. "Awe man." they started to explain that in their rush they had left their phones and everything in the rain. They just knew that they were going to get it for that.

Just as they were about to explain, Sandra shouted out to them, "Hey guys, nice fish!" There on the big porch next to Justin's sister, their bike and gear all safe and dry. What the … both boys ran up to see their haul. A stringer of fish, trout, hung from Roberts bike handle bars. Justin moved to his bike to see his backpack flipped open. Inside peaking their head out was a bouquet of jasmine flowers. He smiled and took one out and gave it to his sister. He grabbed the rest and ran out to his mom handing her what was left. Let's go home folks it's been a long night, the sheriff instructed.

The boys ran and got their bikes and headed home with their families. The boys turned back to look at the house and the pier confused at all the nights events. There was a fire truck at the pier. What's up down there Robert asked his mom. She quickly told him that a freak water spout hit the pier and tore it up! The boys shot each other a knowing look. The families parted ways on the street in front of their houses. Both boys went into their rooms after putting their bikes and fish away. They both must have been asleep before they hit their beds!

The morning light shown its face through Justin's room. He Woke up looking slowly around … As usual he heard his family chattering in the kitchen. He got up, looked in the mirror and combed his hair and headed to the kitchen. He was just thinking "Man what a dream!", but as he got closer to the kitchen… there was that smell again. There on the counter in a vase was the jasmine from the dream! Was it real, he looked around confused?

They talked about the events of last night. Justin never told of the woman or man in that garden that night, nor did he tell of being caught in the cellar. Late that evening he walked down to the mansion leaving a jasmine flower on the porch and whispering, "Thank you for saving us!!" As he walked by the grave under the oak tree, he saw the jasmine bush filled with flowers.

A knowing smile came across his face. "Thank you." He whispered again.

THE END

# BIG MYSTERY OF BAYSPORT

Characters:
Justin, Sandra, Tom, Mom
1st Friend------------------------------------------------Robert
2nd, 3rd, and 4th, friends are boys met in neighborhood.
Sherriff of BaysPort
Pirate-------------------------------------------------------
Captain
Daughter--------------------------------------------------Cindy

## Credits to:

I would like to thank my good friend Dianna P. and her mother for the three day use of her cabin to complete this book. I would also like to thank my sister Tammy P. for editing and typing this book for me.

Also thanking my own family for their contributions, and the Town I live in for inspiration.

# ABOUT THE AUTHOR
# BONNIE HOWELL-LUTTON

A native Texan, with a lifelong dream of becoming an author. She has worked in the Educational field for the past twenty years. The Special Educational department has been her passion. Bonnie moved to the small south Texas coastal town of Fulton Texas fifteen years ago to fulfill one of her dreams of living by the sea. This proved to be the perfect inspirational spot for her to start her lifelong dream of writing. Without the help of her sister and close friend none of this would have been possible. She hopes that you will enjoy reading the "BIG MYSTERY OF BAYSPORT" as much She enjoyed writing it.

Printed in the United States
By Bookmasters